Shirley Barber's Fairy Collection

Table of Contents

The enchanting picture books of bestselling author/illustrator Shirley Barber are loved by children around the world. After growing up in the Channel Islands she and her family came to Australia. Her books, with their exquisite illustrations of fairy folk and woodland creatures, have been delighting children and parents alike for more than a decade.

BEDTIME STORIES

The Royal Jewellers

Under the hedge by a big green field stood a tiny shop called: 'Edwin Beetle & Son, Jewellers.' If you knelt down and peered through the window you could see Mr Beetle and his son Benny working in the shop while Mrs Beetle cooked the meals and looked after weeny Baby Beetle, asleep in his nutshell cradle.

The Beetles lived very comfortably until one day a huge red tractor started to plough up the green field beside their shop. The Beetles, terrified, packed up the few things they could carry and fled till they reached the forests of Fairyland.

"If we aren't safe living in Fairyland," said Mrs Beetle firmly, "well, I don't know where we can go, indeed I don't!" So, among the twisted roots of a large tree, they set up their tiny new shop with their home behind it.

At first, very few customers stopped to look at the necklaces and rings. Mr Beetle would sadly shake his head, remembering the nice shop and home he had once had. Nothing would ever be the same again, he thought.

Then, one day, a beautiful golden fairy stopped and looked at the tiny shop in surprise. She knelt down so she could see better, and Mr Beetle and Benny proudly showed her their finest jewellery.

"These are wonderfully made," said the golden fairy. "Your work is so fine. May I take three necklaces to show the Fairy Queen?"

Mr Beetle made haste to wrap the necklaces in flower petals, tying them into neat parcels with grass blades, and gave them to the fairy. The next day the golden fairy reappeared.

"Mr Beetle, the Queen loves your necklaces and she wants to buy all three," she said smiling. "She offers you three wishes in payment, and she would also like to order a very special tiara, with a matching necklace and bracelet, to be made in gold and many coloured precious gems."

Mr Beetle was at first delighted, but then he became anxious. Where could he get all the gold and different coloured jewels he would need for such an order? "Dearie me!" chuckled Mrs Beetle. "You've got three wishes, haven't you? Wish first for a gold and jewel mine deep beneath this tree, second for a lovely new shop that's big enough to live in too, and third for a food cupboard that fills up again after you've taken things out!"

So that is what he did. Now, a quaint little shop stands among the twisted tree roots. Inside, Mr Beetle is always busy at his workbench, while Mrs Beetle looks after Baby Beetle, and cooks such delicious treats that there is nearly always a visitor dropping in for a chat and a slice of freshly baked cake. And every time Mr Beetle needs another diamond or an emerald or a gold nugget, Benny nips down the tunnel to the mine below.

Whenever anyone is sad about their life, Mrs Beetle simply smiles and says, "Never give up hope! Look at us! We lost everything, then overnight things changed and here we are better off than we ever were before!"

5

The Unicorns

$\mathcal{A}$mong the golden hills of Fairyland, the unicorns run wild and free among the buttercups, with the sunlight flashing from their golden hooves and horns.

One Midsummer Day, the sun was shining and a warm breeze was blowing, but there was a restless, unsettled air about the unicorns.

"Mother," said a young foal, whose name was Ivory, "Everything seems strange today. Is something unusual about to happen?"

"Yes, dear," replied Moonbeam, his mother. "Every Midsummer Day the fairy people use a golden flute to call the unicorns to them, and the fairy children choose one unicorn to live with them for a year."

"Does the unicorn ever come back again?" asked Ivory.

"Oh, yes," his mother replied. "When the fairies choose a new unicorn, they return the one who was chosen the year before. Each unicorn spends a year at the Fairy Palace learning how to be gentle and obedient for the fairy children."

"If they choose me," said Ivory, "I shall say, 'No, I don't want to go.' I want to stay with you, Mother, always."

Moonbeam lifted her head and lovingly nuzzled her young foal. "Dear one, if you are called by the golden flute you can't help but go. It plays a magical note that unicorns can't resist."

Ivory tossed his head and went for a canter, his white mane and tail streaming in the fresh breeze. He was half a hillside away when a distant sweet fluting brought him to a surprised halt. He found he could not help but turn towards it, and soon, quite against his will, he was cantering back to all the other unicorns on the hillside.

There he saw the fairy folk and the flute player for the first time. They were laughing and singing as they made their way along the lane which led up from the lower regions of Fairyland. The fairy children saw Ivory and called joyfully, "That one! Oh, let's choose that one!"

"Not me, Mother!" he pleaded. "Don't let them take me. I don't want to go. It isn't fair!"

Moonbeam gave him a velvet kiss. "Little son, it is an honour to be chosen by the fairies and you must go. We'll soon be together again." Then the fairies placed a garland of flowers around Ivory's neck, and he went with them to Fairyland.

A year passed and once again it was Midsummer Day. Moonbeam stood patiently with the rest of the unicorns as the fairies chose a new unicorn to take to Fairyland. Ivory was released by the fairy children and trotted briskly up to her.

They nuzzled lovingly. Moonbeam said, "You've grown, little son. And was it so bad after all?"

Ivory looked embarrassed. "I missed you, Mother, but I had a really good time, and they told me I was the nicest pet unicorn they ever had."

Then he kicked up his golden heels and galloped away, scattering butterflies and flower petals, and enjoying his freedom once again.

Wilfrid's New Friend

There were two mouse families in Filbert Wood, the Morleys and the Montgomerys. The young mice of both families went to Hollow Log School, but the Montgomery mice were rich and they had scarves and umbrellas for days when it was cold and rainy. The Morley mice, however, had no scarves at all, and only one umbrella between them. So, if it began to rain when Wilfrid Morley Mouse was on his way home from school, he had to wait until it stopped, or until his mother came with the umbrella.

One day it began to rain so Wilfrid ran to a hollow at the foot of a nearby tree and sat down to wait. Presently, Milly Montgomery Mouse and her brother Milford came past under their umbrellas.

"Who got his whiskers wet because he hasn't got an umbrella!" jeered Milly.

"Wet whiskers will dry soon enough," said Wilfrid.

"Who only has an old bag to put his homework in instead of a proper schoolbag!" sneered Milford.

"I may not have a smart schoolbag," replied Wilfrid, "but at least I do my own homework!"

Everyone knew Mr Montgomery Mouse did Milford's sums for him, so the brother and sister decided to hurry home before Wilfrid could embarrass them further.

Wilfrid was making himself comfortable on some fallen leaves and practising his tables up to eight times eleven, when suddenly a beautiful fairy dressed in shades of gold ran through the raindrops and arrived at the tree.

"May I shelter here with you until this rain stops?" she asked. The fairy settled herself and put down a small basket of raspberries she had gathered.

"I'm going to make some jam when I get home," she explained, "but we could eat one raspberry each now to help pass the time."

Wilfrid was rather shy at first, never having actually spoken to a fairy before, but by the time they had eaten a raspberry each and joked about the pips, they were feeling like old friends.

Then they played 'I-spy-with-my-little-eye', and later Wilfrid showed the fairy how to play noughts and crosses using the back page of his schoolbook. As they played the rain slowed, and soon Mrs Morley Mouse appeared before them, under her big patched umbrella.

"There now, Wilfy," she chuckled. "Perhaps I needn't have come to meet you after all – the rain has almost stopped." Wilfrid introduced his new friend to his mother, and they talked for a little while until the sun was shining brightly again. Then the fairy said a smiling good-bye to the mice and promised to call by in a few days with a pot of her raspberry jam.

"Well, you are a lucky mouse!" said Wilfrid's mother, "There's not many who get the chance to make friends with a real fairy."

"Yes," agreed Wilfrid, happily. "And do you know what, Mum? If we were rich and I had an umbrella of my own, I would never have met her at all!"

The Fairy Queen's Ruby Pendant

Elissa was Queen Elvira's younger sister. She was a beautiful, impulsive, kindhearted fairy, much loved by the pixies and all the fairy children.

The Queen would often say, "Elissa, you must quieten down. You are a fairy princess, so behave with dignity." Elissa would try to be good for a while, but before she knew it she would be running up the palace staircase again, while the fairy children chased after her with squeals of laughter.

Because of her high spirits, Elissa was often in trouble, and one day something really dreadful happened. The Queen was standing before her mirror admiring her ruby pendant. The ruby was a rare gem with a star glowing in its heart, given to her by the King to wear to the fairy ball.

Suddenly, Elissa burst into the room. She bumped into the Queen and knocked the pendant to the floor, where it broke into two pieces. "Elissa!" cried the Queen. "How could you be so clumsy! The ruby is ruined!"

The Queen was very upset. Elissa crept around like a mouse and wept. She knew she would not be allowed to go to the ball.

The day of the ball dawned and the fairy children came running to find their favourite playmate. "Come to the seashore with us, Elissa," they cried. "The tide is very low today, and we can see jewels in the rock pools just waiting for us to pick them up."

Elissa still felt sad but she was too kindhearted to refuse the children, so together they set off for the seashore. In spite of her sadness, she joined in the search and before long she spotted a magnificent gem. "Oh, look!" she cried. It was a ruby with a double star in its heart, the rarest of all gems to be found in Fairyland! Elissa hurried back to the palace and asked to see the King.

"Your Majesty," said Elissa respectfully, "I have found this beautiful gem and hope you will take it to give to my sister in place of the pendant I broke."

The King gasped at the beauty of the stone. "This is the finest jewel I've ever seen," he said. "This certainly makes amends for your clumsiness!"

Soon a new glittering double-starred pendant was presented to the Queen. The King explained where the beautiful jewel came from.

"Oh, Elissa," cried the Queen. "It is the most beautiful ruby. All is forgiven and forgotten – and of course you must come to the ball tonight!"

"Hooray!" shouted Elissa. She rushed out of the room, pursued by the fairy children, and the sound of her feet flying up the palace stairway could plainly be heard. The King and Queen looked at each other and smiled. Elissa hadn't changed – but perhaps they didn't really want her to!

Elfrin and the Baby Bluebird

It was the day before the Fairyland Flower Festival. The fairyfolk were in the fields and woodlands picking flowers to make wreaths and garlands.

Netta took her baby brother, Elfrin, with her to the blossom woods. Elfrin could walk and talk quite well, but he was not very good at flying yet, and he still needed an afternoon sleep.

Netta and Elfrin joined the other fairyfolk for a picnic lunch under the trees. Later, she found a hollow under a shady fern, made a nice nest of soft moss, and tucked her baby brother up in it. "Now, go to sleep, little one," she told him, "and I'll come back to fetch you at tea-time."

As soon as Netta had gone, Elfrin opened his eyes, climbed out of his bed and toddled off. He had not gone very far when he heard some tweeting in a large bush.

He looked up and saw a baby bluebird flapping wildly on the edge of a nest. Suddenly it fell and landed on the soft moss in front of Elfrin.

"You naughty birdie," scolded Elfrin, "You should be sleeping in bed." He picked up the baby bird, puffing and panting, and lugged it back to his own nest under the fern.

"Now, go to sleep, little one," he said firmly, just like Netta, and off he toddled again.

Meanwhile, Mr. and Mrs. Bluebird fluttered back to their nest – and found the baby had gone! They flew into a panic, tweeting loudly, terrified that harm had come to their baby. They flew through the trees until they came to the nearest of the fairies – which happened to be Netta.

"Calm down," she told them. "Your baby can't be very far. I'll help you look for it."

Meanwhile, Elfrin had arrived back at the bluebirds' nest. He wondered if there were any more baby birds in it, so he climbed all the way up and out along a branch until he reached the nest. It was empty, but it was so cosy that Elfrin thought he would try it out. He climbed in and quickly fell asleep.

In the other nest under the fern, the baby bluebird sat up and began loudly tweeting for its parents. Netta and the bluebirds followed its tweets to the fern-shaded nest Netta had made for her brother earlier.

"Well, here is your baby – but where is my baby brother?" cried Netta, now rather worried herself.

"I wonder if…?" she murmured, then she flew off to the bush where the bluebirds had their nest. There she found her little brother fast asleep.

"What have you been up to, Elfrin?" laughed Netta. Elfrin opened his big blue eyes and yawned. "Tea-time?" he asked his sister.

"Yes, tea-time," smiled Netta. "And the bluebirds want their nest back, so unless you want earthworms for tea like a baby bluebird, you had better come home with me!"

Lost in the Forest

"Now, children," said Mrs Rabbit one sunny afternoon, "I want you to go to Granny's burrow and give her a bottle of my violet cough syrup. When you arrive at the crossroads, take the path marked 'Primrose Lane', and that will lead you to Granny's home. But if you see those two Ratling brothers, don't stop to play with them because you know they're always getting into mischief!"

Off went Bobtail and Fluffkin, but when they reached the crossroads who should they see but the two naughty young rats leaning against the signpost. Bobtail hurried his sister Fluffkin along the path marked 'Primrose Lane', and away from the Ratlings who jeered and whistled rudely after them.

They soon reached Granny's burrow and she welcomed them with kisses and afternoon tea.

Granny was glad to have the cough syrup because she had a tickling cough on cold nights.

When it was time for them to return home, Granny told them how to find their way. "Now, when you reach the crossroads, take the path marked 'Cowslip Warren'," she said, "and then you will soon be safely home."

When Bobtail and Fluffkin arrived at the crossroads, they were glad to see the two rats had gone. "This sign says 'Cowslip Warren'," Bobtail told his sister, "and so that is our way home."

But soon they became worried. The path they were following seemed to be leading them deeper into the forest instead of home. Bobtail stopped. "Fluffkin, this must be the wrong path," he said. "I think we're lost. We must find a hole to spend the night, and tomorrow, when it's light, we'll try to find our way home."

But Bobtail couldn't find a hole deep enough to hide in, and he could hear a fox barking in the distance. Fluffkin was so frightened that she trembled.

Suddenly a beautiful blue fairy appeared before them holding a sparkling wand in her hand.

"Don't be afraid," she said. "I will use my magic to send the fox away on a long hunt, and I will teach those naughty Ratling brothers a lesson.

"They turned the signpost round so you would take the wrong path. That's why you became lost."

"And as for you, little bunnies, I will light my bluebell lamps and show you the way home!"

"Oh, thank you, kind fairy," chorused the little rabbits. Off they ran along the path towards home. The fairy's bluebell lamps lit up just ahead of them all the way, until they ran into the arms of their mother and father who were waiting for them at their own front door. After such an adventure in the dark forest they were safely home once more!

The
ENCHANTED WOODS

Once upon a time, a little girl called Sarah Jane lived in a pretty cottage at the edge of a wood. The trees in the wood grew close together and on hot days she liked to sit in the shade and play with her toys.

There were ferns and flowers growing thickly between the trees and patches of wild strawberry plants. One warm sunny day, Sarah Jane wandered into the woods to play with her toys and look for wild strawberries.

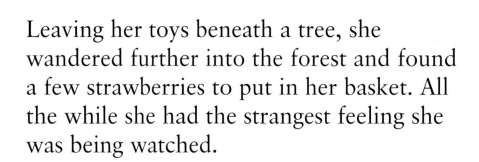

Leaving her toys beneath a tree, she wandered further into the forest and found a few strawberries to put in her basket. All the while she had the strangest feeling she was being watched.

Eventually, she came to a big old tree and under the tree was a ring of mushrooms.

It was a magic fairy ring. But Sarah Jane didn't see it until after she had stepped inside. She stared at it, puzzled, and wondered what it was.

Suddenly Sarah Jane glimpsed a procession of fairies winding through the trees. Some were quaint and impish and others were the most beautiful creatures she had ever seen.

"Sarah Jane," they cried, "you are needed in Fairyland. Now that we've caught you in our magic fairy ring we can take you with us."

Then they waved their magic wands, and Sarah Jane felt herself become smaller and smaller.

She was now no taller than the fairies, and felt as light as thistledown. The fairies took her gently by the hands, and together they flew up above the treetops and out over a shimmering sea.

They landed on the shores of a strange and beautiful land. The flowers were taller than they were, and huge butterflies waited to greet them.

Soon, a messenger arrived from the fairy palace.

"Sarah Jane," he announced, "the Fairy King and Queen have been told of your arrival, and they would like to see you now."

So the fairies sat Sarah Jane on the back of a butterfly, and together they flew over a lake to the fairy palace, whose golden turrets sparkled in the morning sunlight.

The King and Queen welcomed Sarah Jane, and told her why she was needed in Fairyland.

"Our daughter is to be married to a prince from a neighbouring kingdom," said the Queen. "We need the presence of a mortal to ensure their good fortune and a happy marriage."

"Yes," said the King. "You will bring them good luck. Come, you will be our honoured guest and join us in our celebration."

Soon, it was time for the
wedding. The chatter and laughter
of the guests grew quiet as they
gathered to watch the Prince and Princess
exchange wedding vows.

After the wedding, a magnificent banquet was held in a glittering hall overlooking the lake. Sweet music was played by a band of funny little musicians while everyone, including Sarah Jane, feasted on the finest delicacies Fairyland could offer.

When the banquet was over, it was time for the Prince and Princess to leave. Together, they descended the golden stairway, as their guests cheered and showered them with rose petals. Then they climbed into a golden carriage drawn by dragonflies and flew off to their new home over the hills.

Now it was time for Sarah Jane to return home, too. The fairies flew with her over the sea and back to the fairy ring in the woods. They waved their magic wands, and once again she became her normal size.

"Goodbye, Sarah Jane," they said, dropping feather-light kisses upon her cheek. "You will always be our special friend."

Then she found herself alone in the woods once more with her basket and her toys beneath the shady tree.

Sarah Jane looked at her basket in
amazement. It was overflowing with small,
delicious strawberries. She picked up the
basket and her toys and wandered home.
Her family found it hard to believe her
wonderful tale of how she had been a guest
at a fairy wedding. But certainly, no one
had ever seen so many wild strawberries as
she had in her basket. They agreed that it
must be a gift to her from the fairies, a sign
to show she really *had* been to Fairyland.

RAINBOW MAGIC

Once upon a time,
there was an old lady called Gran Tibbett.
She lived in a farmhouse on the edge of the
forest with her granddaughter Annie and Little
Dog Bozo. Around the house was a pretty rose
garden, and around the garden was a grassy
meadow that went right to the edge
of the dark Fern Forest.

Early in the morning
the deer and their fawns would come out
of the forest and eat the grass in the meadow.
Sometimes Annie could get quite close to a fawn,
but Little Dog Bozo would run out and
bark at the big deer.
"One day they won't run away,"
Annie scolded. "Then you'll be sorry."
But Little Dog Bozo only laughed.

When the weather turned cold, Gran Tibbet's knee-joints stiffened and her elbows creaked, and everything that could ache began to ache. She would sigh and sadly say to Annie and Little Dog Bozo, "I'm getting old, and I'm good and ready for my Heavenly Reward. But who will look after you when I'm gone?"

But Annie and Little Dog Bozo were
not really worried because they felt sure Gran
would go on being Gran forever. They built
houses of dried fern fronds and made leaf boats,
and sailed them on the still water. A big fish lived
in the pool and if they kept very still, he rose to
look at them. But Bozo always barked and with a
splash the fish would be gone again.

On showery days, Annie sometimes saw a rainbow so close she called to Gran, "Shall I run to see if I can find the fairies' pot of gold at the end of the rainbow?" But Gran said, "You keep away from rainbows, Annie, They are very funny things. You can get caught under rainbows, and never come home again."

One day, when Annie and Little Dog Bozo were playing in the forest, it began to rain. They crept into a hollow tree. Soon the sun shone again, and suddenly a big, beautiful rainbow came curving out of the sky and touched the mossy ground in front of them. Just inside the rainbow was a pot filled with gold.

"Oh," cried Annie, "What a lovely present to take to Gran!" She forgot all about Gran's warning and ran towards the pot. But as she and Little Dog Bozo went under the rainbow something very strange happened. They started to shrink and became smaller and smaller until they turned into…two little Fairy Folk! They each now had wings and were so small that the grass blades were as tall to them as trees.

"Oh, Bozo!" cried Annie, "How will we find our way home to Gran to tell her what has happened to us?" She sat down under a toadstool and began to cry.

Bozo tried out his wings,
but landed head-over-paws in a clump
of violets. Annie couldn't help laughing.
"We'll have to walk until we learn to fly,"
she said. "Come on, let's go home."

After a while they came to a deep river. "How
shall we get across?" whispered Annie to Bozo.
Just then a frog came out from his moss-covered
house and offered to ferry them across the water.
"What a nice boat!" Annie said as she climbed
in. "It reminds me of something. Why, I do
believe it's one of the boats we made
when we were playing here."
When they reached the other bank Annie
thanked the frog and gave him a
biscuit from her lunch bag.

The sun went down and the forest filled with shadows. Annie and Little Dog Bozo began to feel frightened. Suddenly, a family of mice came scurrying along the path, scaring Bozo. But the mice were friendly and warned the two new Fairy Folk that the big wild cat was out hunting.

"Hurry, he's coming," they said. "Follow us."

So Annie and Little Dog Bozo went home with the mice for supper. They had grasshopper pie and toasted midges, and Annie broke up some biscuits to give to the baby mice. Then they all went to sleep, tucked up small and warm in a soft bed of thistledown. When the moon rose the mice ran out to dance in the moonlight, but Annie and Little Dog Bozo did not wake till sunrise.

The next morning, Annie and Bozo
said goodbye to the mice and set off on their long
walk home. After a while, they rested with some
friendly bluebirds they met on their way.
They ate moth cakes and ant cookies, and
drank tea out of flower cups. Then they all sat on
a wild rose branch and sang some songs until it was
time for them to set off once more on
their journey home.

The next day they met a wise old
Mr. Longlegs who knew almost everything
about everything. After they had told him their
story, he looked at them thoughtfully for a
while, then said:

"I think you had better meet the Fairy King
and Queen and all the other Fairy Folk. Little folk
just like yourselves live in the ferny glade by the
waterfall just down the path."

Annie and Little Dog Bozo felt so
happy to know there were other little people
just like themselves!

They thanked Mr. Longlegs and ran towards
the waterfall which sparkled between the trees.
But suddenly, that wicked wild cat pounced on
Little Dog Bozo and was about
to eat him when…

"Stop that at once," a voice commanded. "Put down that fairy person!" It was the Fairy King. The cat sulkily put down Little Dog Bozo and slunk away. Then the Fairy King led them to the Fairy Court where they met the Fairy Queen.

In the ferny glade were gathered all those who had gone under rainbows at one time or another. The King explained that because Annie and Bozo had not listened to Gran Tibbet's warning they would now be Fairy Folk for ever and ever. They must learn to be good Fairy Folk just like the others. Then all the fairies, elves and pixies came forward to greet them.

So Annie and Little Dog Bozo
lived happily with the fairies, but they longed
to see Gran again. One day they asked the
King and Queen if they could visit her and
soon all the court were winging their way
through the fern forest till they came to Gran
Tibbet's old, old house.

Gran was sitting in the twilight, feeling very
sad. She had given up all hope of ever seeing
Annie and Little Dog Bozo again.
Suddenly she looked up and saw a tiny little
Annie and a weeny Little Dog Bozo alight upon
her verandah rail. Behind them all the fairies
fluttered down to picnic in her rose garden.

"Look, Gran," cried Annie, "we're safe
after all, but we have to be Fairy Folk for ever
and ever. We're well and happy, and we've
brought a present for you – the pot of gold
we found under the rainbow."

So Annie and Little Dog Bozo lived with the
Fairy Folk forever, but they often came to talk to
Gran while the Fairy Court picnicked in her rose
garden. Gran stopped worrying about who
would take care of Annie and Little Dog
Bozo because she knew that now they
could look after themselves.

And what about the pot of gold? Of course it was only a fairy-sized pot of gold, so Gran set it on her mantelpiece in a tiny glass case, just to prove that fairy folk really *did* live in the Fern Forest and that there really *was* a pot of gold to be found under the rainbow.

THE TOOTH FAIRY

Tom had a loose tooth. It fell out while he and his sister Holly were playing in the garden.

"Don't lose it," said Holly. "We'll put it in a glass of water. Then tonight we'll wait for the Tooth Fairy to come and collect it."

So Tom put the tooth in his pocket. But when he looked for it at tea-time it had vanished.

After tea, Tom and Holly took a torch and went into the garden to search for the lost tooth, but it was nowhere to be found. Tired and disappointed, they went to bed.

"Now we'll *never* see the Tooth Fairy," sighed Holly, "Last time, when I lost a tooth, I tried so hard to stay awake, but I couldn't. The Tooth Fairy took my tooth, left some money behind, and was gone. I didn't see a thing!"

That night, the children slept soundly. Just as the sun was rising, Tom was woken by a tinkling in the kitchen. He tiptoed in and saw the Tooth Fairy sitting on the window sill.

"Tom," she said softly, "you must search for your missing tooth – it's very important indeed. If you and Holly can find it, I promise to show you my home in the clouds and tell you why I need your tooth."

So Tom woke up Holly, and together they ran out into the garden.

Frantically they searched for the missing tooth. At last, they found it, shining white amongst the daisies.

"Hooray!" laughed the Tooth Fairy. "Now I'll take you to Cloudland, just as I promised."

She waved her magic wand, and suddenly
Holly and Tom were as small as the Tooth
Fairy. But before they had time to be
surprised, she waved her wand again and
white doves began to swoop down from
the trees. They had golden bridles and
red velvet saddles.

"Jump on, Holly!" cried Tom. "We're
going for a ride – up into the sky!'

The white doves flew high into the pink dawn sky where amongst the clouds lay a magical land with hills as soft as cotton wool.

They landed beside a beautiful palace surrounded by gardens full of the strangest plants the children had ever seen.

There were silver stars growing like flowers, and tended by pixie gardeners, and moored by a cloud was a boat with rainbow sails.

"Now, Holly and Tom," said the Tooth Fairy, "the stars in the sky eventually grow old and fall down, and the fairies must replace them.

"New stars grow from special star seeds, which are children's baby teeth. That is why when a child's tooth drops out I come down and collect it!"

"But why is my tooth so important?" asked Tom.

"Well," said the Tooth Fairy, "most stars in the sky are silver, but here and there you can see gold ones.

"Now, *your* teeth are very special, Tom, because they will grow into golden stars. And we know an old golden star will fall very soon, and will need to be replaced."

"Look!" cried Holly, "A golden star is falling now!"

"Come, children!" said the Tooth Fairy, taking their hands. "It's time to replace the old golden star. We must hurry and plant Tom's tooth in the sky!"

A silver boat was moored not far from the house. The Tooth Fairy and the children climbed aboard and together they set sail into the sky until they reached the place where the golden star had been.

"Please may I plant my own tooth?" asked Tom.

"Of course," said the Tooth Fairy, and she showed Tom what to do.

The silver boat sailed back to Cloudland, and the Tooth Fairy and the children jumped out onto the clouds. "Soon you must go home," said the Tooth Fairy, "but first come into my house and have some breakfast."

A bell tinkled and all the pixie gardeners came scampering inside to join them. They all had breakfast together. Then the Tooth Fairy waved her magic wand and...

Tom found he was back in his bed! Holly came running into his room. "Tom!" she said excitedly. "Did we really see the Tooth Fairy last night? Or was it a dream?"

"It's true!" laughed Tom. "The Tooth Fairy took us with her to Cloudland!" Then they ran to tell their parents.

That night Tom and Holly searched the sky for a glittering new golden star. "Look!" cried Tom, at last. "There it is! That's the one I planted! My very own golden star!"

95

The Five Mile Press

The Five Mile Press Pty Ltd
950 Stud Road, Rowville
Victoria 3178 Australia
Email: publishing@fivemile.com.au
Website: www.fivemile.com.au

First published in 2001
Reprinted 2002 (twice), 2003 (twice), 2004 (twice), 2005 (three times), 2006

Copyright © 2001 Marbit Pty Ltd
www.shirleybarbers.com
Text and illustrations by Shirley Barber
CD produced by Stephanie Mann and Spoken Word Productions
This collection copyright © 2001 The Five Mile Press Pty Ltd

Printed in China

National Library of Australia
Cataloguing-in-Publication data
Barber, Shirley
Shirley Barber's fairy collection.
ISBN 1 86503 572 6
1. Fairies - Juvenile fiction. I. Title
A823.3